MARMADUKE
and the Scary Story

Story by Michael Ratnett
Illustrations by June Goulding

Mini Treasures

RED FOX

For Princess, Mouse, Pip and Topsey Rabbit

1 3 5 7 9 0 8 6 4 2

Copyright © text Michael Ratnett 1990
Copyright © illustrations June Goulding 1990

Michael Ratnett and June Goulding have asserted their right
under the Copyright, Designs and Patents Act, 1988
to be identified as the author and illustrator of this work.

First published in the United Kingdon 1990
by Hutchinson Children's Books

First published in Mini Treasures edition 1998
by Red Fox
Random House, 20 Vauxhall Bridge Road,
London, SW1V 2SA

Random House Australia (Pty) Ltd
20 Alfred Street, Milsons Point, Sydney,
New South Wales 2061, Australia

Random House New Zealand Limited
18 Poland Road Glenfield,
Auckland 10, New Zealand

Random House South Africa
PO Box 2263, Rosebank 2121, South Africa

RANDOM HOUSE UK Limited Reg No. 954009

A CIP catalogue record for this book
is available from the British library.

Printed in Singapore

ISBN 0 09 926346 7

Marmaduke, Jessica and Harriet were all very excited. Grandma and Grandpa were coming to stay.

'Stop fidgeting,' said Dad. 'Go and do something.'

'Yes,' said Mum. 'Why not paint them a picture as a surprise?'

'Wow,' said Marmaduke, as the
rabbits raced up to their room.
'What a great idea! I'll paint them
a wonderful picture!'

'And so will I,' said Jessica.

'Me too,' said Harriet.

Soon they were very busy.
   'No peeping!' said Marmaduke.

When they came back down, they showed each other their pictures.

Jessica had painted a picture of a butterfly...

Harriet had painted a picture of a flower...

And Marmaduke had painted a picture of a MONSTER!

'Oh Marmaduke,' said Mum, 'why couldn't you paint something nice like the others?'

'Pooh!' said Marmaduke. 'Nice things are no fun. I like *scary* things!'

'Look what we've got for you!' said the three small rabbits as soon as Grandma and Grandpa arrived.

'Why, what lovely pictures,' they said. 'We can't think which one we like the best!'

Then they all sat down to tea.
Grandpa had *eleven* biscuits.
  'Doesn't Grandpa eat a lot!'
whispered Jessica.

'It's called being greedy,' said Grandma.

After tea Jessica said, 'Tell us a story, Grandpa.'

'Of course I will,' he said. 'But I'll just have one more biscuit first.'

'Tell them a story *now*,' said Grandma. 'You've had quite enough biscuits for one day.'

'What sort of story would you like?'
asked Grandpa.

'A SCARY story!' said
Marmaduke.

So they huddled around, and
Grandpa told them a scary story
about a monster with three legs, just
like the one in Marmaduke's picture.

'Time for bed,' said Dad.

And they were monsters all the way
up the stairs.

It was a dark and windy night.

'What did you think of Grandpa's story?' said Jessica.

'It was a very scary story,' said Harriet

'Yes,' said Marmaduke, 'but I wasn't afraid. Were you?'

'No,' said Jessica.

'Of course not,' said Harriet.

But they couldn't go to sleep.

Suddenly Jessica said, 'W-what's that noise?'

'What noise?' said Harriet.

'Th‑ that's just the wind,' said Marmaduke.

'Or‑ or a tree branch tapping,' said Harriet.

They listened again.

'It's not,' said Jessica. 'It's coming from the stairs!'

'W‑ what shall we do,' said Harriet. I'm scared!'

'One of you must go and look,' said Marmaduke.

'You go and look,' said Jessica.
'You're the one who likes scary
things!'

'All right, we'll all go together,'
said Marmaduke.

Shivering from the tips of their
ears to the ends of their toes, they
climbed out of bed and crept
towards the door. Marmaduke went
in front firmly grasping his
cricket bat.

When they were on the landing, they looked down. There, coming up the stairs was a huge shadowy figure! Thump, thump, click it went. Thump, thump, click...

'It's the three - legged monster!' stammered Marmaduke. And he raised his cricket bat way up high...

...and hit the monster thwack on the head!

'Ow!!' yelled Grandpa.

Then the light came on.

'What is all that noise?' said Dad.

'Marmaduke hit me on the head!'
said Grandpa.

'We thought he was a monster!'
said Marmaduke.

'Well, he is *sometimes*,' said
Grandma, 'especially when he creeps
about after biscuits.'
And they all laughed.

Mum made everyone a mug of steaming cocoa and sent the three small rabbits back to bed.

'I still think you were very brave, Marmaduke,' said Jessica.

'I do too,' said Harriet, 'even though Grandpa wasn't really a monster.'

But Marmaduke was busy.

'ROAR!' he screamed!